The Lions

Ladybird Books Loughborough

Once upon a time it rained and rained.
There was so much water that Mr Noah
made a boat.

The boat was called an ark.
All the animals went to live on this ark
with Mr Noah.

Mr Noah counted the animals.
They went into the ark two by two.

One day the two lions said,
"Let's have some fun."

"I know what we can do,"
said one lion. "Come with me."

The lions found some black paint.

Soon Mr Noah looked at his clock.
''It's time for tea,'' he said.

"Tea time!" he shouted,
and the animals came.
Mr Noah counted . . . two elephants

. . . two ostriches . . .

10

two horses . . .

two monkeys

. . . two little mice . . .

two green snakes . . .

three tigers and one lion.

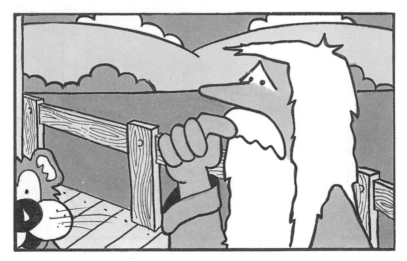

"That's not right," said Mr Noah.
"There should be two tigers, not three."

Then it started to rain.
''We must go inside,'' said Mr Noah.

"Go inside, animals," he said,
and they all went inside for tea.

"Look at all that rain," said Mr Noah,
and he closed the door.

15

"Eat your tea, animals," he said.
There were bananas for the monkeys,
carrots for the rabbits,

and some hay for the horses.

Mr Noah had cakes and some tea.
Then there was a knock on the door.

It was one of the lions.
He was very wet and black paint was
dripping off him.

"So that is why I had **three** tigers,"
said Mr Noah. All the animals laughed.

The two lions had tea.
''We won't play any more tricks
on Mr Noah,'' they said.

The Snake

"It will be a nice day today,"
said Mr Noah. "I'll have a Sports Day
for the animals."

He painted white lines for the
running races.

He put up a big pole for the high jump.

He put some sand for the long jump,

and a big table for cakes and lemonade.

Mr Noah said to the animals,
''Today we will have our Sports Day.''
''Hooray!'' they all shouted.

"The first race will be a running race,"
said Mr Noah.

He put up his hand and said,
"One, two, three, **go**!"

The animals ran and ran and
the tiger won the race.
"Well done, tiger!" said Mr Noah.

The next race was an egg and spoon race.

"One, two, three, **go**!" said Mr Noah . . .
and off they went.

But the rabbit broke his egg.
All the animals laughed.

The monkey fell over and lost his egg.

So the ostrich won the race.
"Well done, ostrich!" said Mr Noah.

There were lots and lots of races
all day.
The animals had lots of fun.

A horse won the sack race.

The rabbit won the high jump.

And a big, strong gorilla won the weight lifting.

In this race was the lion, the bear, the giraffe and . . . the little green snake.

"One, two, three, **go**!" shouted Mr Noah.

First they ran to some boxes. They had
to get over the top of the boxes.

The giraffe had long legs. He was first to get over the top.

The little green snake went as fast as he could.

Then they came to a ladder. The giraffe got his legs stuck.

The lion and the bear were soon at the top. The little green snake went as fast as he could.

Then they had to come down the
ladder. All the animals shouted.

"Come on, lion! Come on, bear!
Come on, little green snake!"

Next they had to go through
some rings.

The lion got through but the bear
was too big.

He got stuck! The little green snake
went as fast as he could.

"Come on, lion! Come on, snake!"
shouted all the animals.

In the last part of the race, they had to get under a big net.

The lion went first, but he got stuck.

"Come on, snake!" said the tortoise.
"You can win, snake," said Mr Noah.

"I can win the race," said the snake,
"but I have to get under the big net."

43

Then the little snake made himself into a ball and went under the net.

He came first. The little snake had won the race.

"Hooray!" shouted the animals.
"Well done!" said Mr Noah.

45

Then it was time to give the prizes to all the winners.

A cup for
the gorilla.

A cup for
the rabbit.

"And this big cup is for the snake,"
said Mr Noah. "It's for the best race
of the day."

Then the animals helped Mr Noah.
The monkeys put away the poles.

The ostriches put away the rings.

The elephant helped Mr Noah, too.

Then the animals had their tea and
soon it was time for bed.

The little green snake went to bed.

He was very happy.
''I like Sports Day,'' he said.

Notes to parents and teachers

This series of books is designed for children who have begun to read and who need, and will enjoy, wider reading at a supplementary level.

The stories are based on Key Words up to *Level 5c* of the Ladybird Key Words Reading Scheme.

Extra words and words beyond that level are listed below.

Words which the child will meet at *Level 6* are listed separately, in case the parent or teacher wishes to give extra attention to these words and use this series as a bridge between reading levels.

Although based on Key Words, these books are ideal as supplementary reading material for use with any other reading scheme. The high picture content gives visual clues to words which may be unfamiliar and the consistent repetition of new words will give confidence to the reader.

Words used at Level 6

Mr	green	wet
time	three	today
live	door	next
day	very	egg